NELLIE and the BANDIT

Eileen Ross

PICTURES BY
Erin E. Kono

Farrar Straus Giroux • New York

To Dad, who took me to the library on Saturdays   —E.R.

For Mom and Dad —E.E.K.

Text copyright © 2005 by Eileen Ross
Illustrations copyright © 2005 by Erin Eitter Kono
Distributed in Canada by Douglas & McIntyre Publishing Group
Color separations by Chroma Graphics PTE Ltd.
Printed and bound in the United States of America by Berryville Graphics
Typography by Nancy Goldenberg
First edition, 2005
10 9 8 7 6 5 4 3 2 1

www.fsgkidsbooks.com

Library of Congress Cataloging-in-Publication Data
Ross, Eileen, date.
    Nellie and the bandit / Eileen Ross ; pictures by Erin Eitter Kono.— 1st ed.
        p.   cm.
    Summary: When Desperado Dan breaks out of jail, Nellie sets out to find
her pa, the sheriff, but finds the outlaw first.
    ISBN-13: 978-0-374-35508-1
    ISBN-10: 0-374-35508-8
    [1. Robbers and outlaws—Fiction.   2. West (U.S.)—Fiction.   3. Sex
role—Fiction.]   I. Kono, Erin Eitter, ill.   II. Title.

PZ7.R719646Ne 2005
[E]—dc22

                                        2003054159

N ellie scurried toward the telegraph office, where commotion was spilling onto the street like a tipped-over bottle of sarsaparilla.

"Desperado Dan has escaped from jail," the clerk, Ned Jenkins, hollered while hammering a WANTED poster to the door.

As Nellie crowded in to get a closer look, she noticed Miz Witherspoon, the schoolmarm, looking lumpy and gray as the breakfast gruel Nellie had cooked up on the iron stove for Pa that very morning.

"Rosie's missing," Miz Witherspoon wailed. "I can't find my poor sweet mule anywhere."

"We've got ourselves an outlaw on the loose!" the mayor replied. "No time to worry about wandering mules now."

And that's when Miz Witherspoon fainted dead away, sinking to the sidewalk like a mudslide after a thunderstorm.

Just then, Ned noticed Nellie. "We're fixin' to form a posse," he said. "Where's your pa?"

"Left for the Cripple Creek Gold Mine right after breakfast," Nellie answered. "Said he'd best check on that old miner, Rooster McGrunt, who never showed up for his weekly bath." But a bothersome thought was tugging away at Nellie's brain. What if Desperado Dan was planning to rob the gold mine? She had to warn Pa!

"I'll fetch him for you," Nellie offered.

The clerk's mouth dropped open. "Why, Nellie Spry! Desperado Dan robs banks and rustles cattle. He's the meanest outlaw in all the West, and you are a mere *girl*! Hurry home and lock the door. Hide under the bed if you must. We'll take care of everything." And off he raced.

With teeth clamped tight to corral her anger, Nellie spun around fast as a Texas tornado. But instead of heading home, she set her sights on the foothills looming in the distance. "A girl, indeed! I'll just have to find Pa before Desperado Dan finds me!" she said, and off she marched toward the Cripple Creek Gold Mine.

After a spell, Nellie came to a fork in the road, where she heard the clip-clop of hooves. She didn't guess most outlaws could read, but she quickly pointed the sign in the wrong direction—just in case. Then she eyed a stranger riding a homely mule she recognized as Rosie.

"Pray tell, what's a purty gal like you doing out alone in the middle of nowhere?" the man asked, as he tumbled down off Rosie.

"Name's Nellie Spry. I'm huntin' my pa so's I can warn him that Desperado Dan's done broke outta jail."

The man snickered like a fox fixin' to raid a chicken house. "Bless my soul! I'm the one they call Desperado Dan. Girl, you best start praying your last."

Nellie stared at the man, then took to laughing. "You stop funnin' me this instant. I know who you are. You're the new preacher man comin' round to take old Reverend Hicklemeyer's place."

She hauled her *McGuffey Reader* from her pocket. "You're welcome to borrow my copy of the Good Book till you get yourself settled, Reverend."

"You think *I'm* a preacher?"

Nellie nodded. "Yep. With that fancy Sunday-go-to-meetin' talk of yours, I reckon ya cain't be nothin' but an honest, God-fearin' man like my pa. Yessir. Follow that sign to the church. There'll be a whole congregation of folks just waitin' for you."

As the man stood puzzling over the sign, Nellie sashayed across the meadow, heading toward a stand of tall pines. She'd heard talk of a shortcut across Dead Man's Bridge and decided to give it a try. Now it was obvious Desperado Dan couldn't read, but was he smart enough to coax Rosie across the rickety bridge above the river?

Nellie didn't ponder the question long, because man and mule soon pulled into sight. "How dull do you think I am, gal?" he asked, as Nellie tippy-toed onto the first wooden slat. "You can't trick me with some dumb sign. I got my training from the greatest masters of all time—Billy the Kid, even Frank and Jesse James."

Nellie stopped halfway across the bridge. "My teacher, Miz Witherspoon, fed us a right hefty dose of readin' and cipherin', but I ain't never heard of them *poets* before." With a loud hee-haw, Rosie plopped down and refused to budge closer to the bridge. The man's face curdled up like milk gone sour in the summer sun. "What rotten excuse for a teacher neglected to teach you American history?" he shouted.

A picture of the frazzled schoolmarm blasted into Nellie's head. "If you ain't the new preacher, you must be the new schoolmaster come to take over for poor Miz Witherspoon."

"Me? A schoolmaster?" The man's voice rose two notches past disbelief. "Girl," he grumbled, shoving Rosie from behind, "when I get this stubborn mule across that bridge, I'll teach you a thing or two!"

"My pa says book learnin' ain't nothin' to be afeared of, and I believe him," Nellie called, after inching her way onto solid ground. "But to my way of thinkin', a body needs a good lick of horse sense, too. Just like that mule has sense enough not to cross this bridge. And me, well, I've got enough sense to be scared of Desperado Dan—if and when I see him."

"You sassy young varmint!" The man sputtered and spit as though his mouth was crammed plumb full of pine needles. "*I* am Desperado Dan," he insisted, tugging on Rosie's reins.

But Nellie didn't pay him any mind.

Instead, she hurried off through the woods, leaving Desperado Dan behind trying to convince Rosie to cross the bridge.

In her haste, Nellie took several wrong turns before finding the right path to the gold mine. She was surprised to hear Desperado Dan's voice bellowing from the trees below. With quickened step, she started climbing the rise toward the gold mine.

"Girl, I'm about to pass sentence on you without so much as a trial," the man hollered, closing in on her. "I'll see you get what's coming to you for all the trouble you've caused me today."

Nellie eyeballed the entrance to the mine, hoping—praying—Pa was still there. "I'm right sorry I offended you," she said, turning to face the stranger. "I promise never to make another mistake like that, Your Honor."

"Did you call me 'Your Honor'?"

"Sure enough did. Took me a heap longer than it should have, but I finally figured out who you are." And with that, Nellie marched toward the entrance, whistling her father's favorite tune as loud as she could.

As the man scuttled along behind, he grumbled at the mule. "Who does she think I am?"

Nellie stopped whistling. "Ain't no question you're a right-minded man like my pa. I figure you're the circuit judge who travels county to county, here to put Desperado Dan back behind bars for robbin' all those banks."

The stranger let loose with a bellyaching wail loud enough to rustle up a rock slide inside the Cripple Creek Gold Mine. "I can't stand it anymore! You've taken me for every rotten thing I can think of," he screeched. "A preacher! A schoolmaster! Even a traveling judge! Why, I swear, gal, the only thing you haven't mistaken me for is the sheriff!"

As Nellie's giggles turned into hoots of laughter, the stranger ripped the hat off his head and stomped it flat. "You'd best tell me what you think is so dad-burned funny, or I'll take care of you once and for all."

Nellie wiped her eyes. "I'm sorry, but I could never mistake *you* for the sheriff."

"And just why not?" he demanded, his voice prickly as a porcupine.

Nellie pointed.

" 'Cause my pa is the sheriff."

Before the man could suck in breath enough to answer, he was lying flat on the ground.

"Why, Nellie, do you know who this man is?" Pa asked.

"Surely do," she replied, nuzzling Rosie's neck. "That's Desperado Dan, meanest outlaw in all the West. Me and Rosie, well, we figured the best way to keep folks safe was to lead him straight here to you."

Nodding proudly, Pa handed Nellie a deputy's star. "That's my girl!"